D1608482

PETER RABBIT™ STORYTIME

TALES FROM BEATRIX POTTER

VOLUME ONE

F. WARNE & Co

FREDERICK WARNE
Published by the Penguin Group
Penguin Books Ltd, 80 Strand, London WC2R 0RL, England
Penguin Young Readers Group, 375 Hudson Street, New York, New York 10014, USA
Penguin Books Australia Ltd, 250 Camberwell Road, Camberwell, Victoria 3124, Australia
Canada, India, New Zealand, South Africa

www.peterrabbit.com

First published by Frederick Warne 2005
3 5 7 9 1 0 8 6 4 2

Printed and bound in Malaysia

Contents

The Tale of Peter Rabbit

1902

About This Book

The story of naughty Peter Rabbit in Mr. McGregor's garden first appeared in a picture letter Beatrix Potter wrote to Noel Moore, the young son of her former governess, in 1893. Encouraged by her success in having some greetings card designs published, Beatrix remembered the letter seven years later, and expanded it into a little picture book, with black-and-white illustrations. It was rejected by several publishers, so Beatrix had it printed herself, to give to family and friends.

About this time, Frederick Warne agreed to publish the tale if the author would supply colour pictures, and the book finally appeared in 1902, priced at one shilling (5p). It was an instant success, and has remained so ever since. A pacy story with an engaging hero, an exciting chase and a happy ending, matched with exquisite illustrations, adds up to a children's classic whose appeal is ageless.

ONCE upon a time there were four little Rabbits, and their names were—

Flopsy,

Mopsy,

Cotton-tail,

and Peter.

They lived with their Mother in a sand-bank, underneath the root of a very big fir-tree.

"Now, my dears," said old Mrs. Rabbit one morning, "you may go into the fields or down the lane, but don't go into Mr. McGregor's garden: your Father had an accident there; he was put in a pie by Mrs. McGregor.

"Now run along, and don't get into mischief. I am going out."

Then old Mrs. Rabbit took a basket and her umbrella, and went through the wood to the baker's. She bought a loaf of brown bread and five currant buns.

Flopsy, Mopsy, and Cotton-tail, who were good little bunnies, went down the lane to gather blackberries.

But Peter, who was very naughty, ran straight away to Mr. McGregor's garden, and squeezed under the gate!

First he ate some lettuces and some French beans; and then he ate some radishes.

And then, feeling rather sick, he went to look for some parsley.

But round the end of a cucumber frame, whom should he meet but Mr. McGregor!

Mr. McGregor was on his hands and knees planting out young cabbages, but he jumped up and ran after Peter, waving a rake and calling out, "Stop thief!"

Peter was most dreadfully frightened; he rushed all over the garden, for he had forgotten the way back to the gate.

He lost one of his shoes among the cabbages, and the other shoe amongst the potatoes.

After losing them, he ran on four legs and went faster, so that I think he might have got away altogether if he had not unfortunately run into a gooseberry net, and got caught by the large buttons on his jacket.

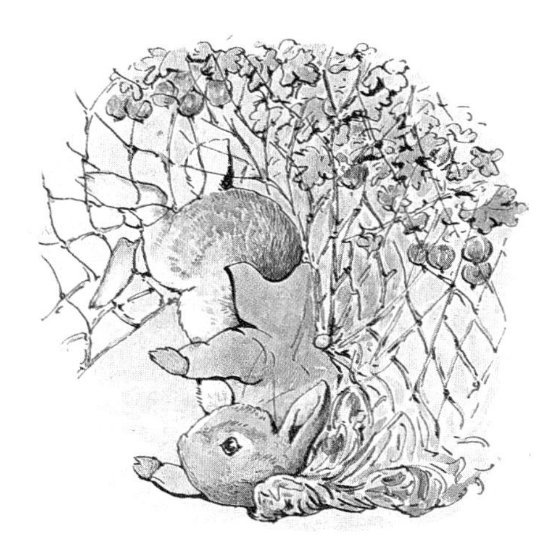

It was a blue jacket with brass buttons, quite new.

Peter gave himself up for lost, and shed big tears; but his sobs were overheard by some friendly sparrows, who flew to him in great excitement, and implored him to exert himself.

Mr. McGregor came up with a sieve, which he intended to pop upon the top of Peter; but Peter wriggled out just in time, leaving his jacket behind him.

And rushed into the tool-shed, and jumped into a can. It would have been a beautiful thing to hide in, if it had not had so much water in it.

Mr. McGregor was quite sure that Peter was somewhere in the tool-shed, perhaps hidden underneath a flower-pot. He began to turn them over carefully, looking under each.

Presently Peter sneezed—"Kertyschoo!" Mr. McGregor was after him in no time.

And tried to put his foot upon Peter, who jumped out of a window, upsetting three plants. The window was too small for Mr. McGregor, and he was tired of running after Peter. He went back to his work.

Peter sat down to rest; he was out of breath and trembling with fright, and he had not the least idea which way to go.

Also he was very damp with sitting in that can.

After a time he began to wander about, going lippity—lippity—not very fast, and looking all round.

He found a door in a wall; but it was locked, and there was no room for a fat little rabbit to squeeze underneath.

An old mouse was running in and out over the stone door-step, carrying peas and beans to her family in the wood. Peter asked her the way to the gate, but she had such a large pea in her mouth that she could not answer. She only shook her head at him. Peter began to cry.

Then he tried to find his way straight across the garden, but he became more and more puzzled. Presently, he came to a pond where Mr. McGregor filled his water-cans. A white cat was staring at some gold-fish, she sat very, very still, but now and then the tip of her tail twitched as if it were alive. Peter thought it best to go away without speaking to her; he had heard about cats from his cousin, little Benjamin Bunny.

He went back towards the tool-shed, but suddenly, quite close to him, he heard the noise of a hoe —scr-r-ritch, scratch, scratch, scritch. Peter scuttered underneath the bushes. But presently, as nothing happened, he came out, and climbed upon a wheelbarrow and peeped over. The first thing he saw was Mr. McGregor hoeing onions. His back was turned towards Peter, and beyond him was the gate!

Peter got down very quietly off the wheelbarrow, and started running as fast as he could go, along a straight walk behind some black-currant bushes.

Mr. McGregor caught sight of him at the corner, but Peter did not care. He slipped underneath the gate, and was safe at last in the wood outside the garden.

Mr. McGregor hung up the little jacket and the shoes for a scarecrow to frighten the blackbirds.

Peter never stopped running or looked behind him till he got home to the big fir-tree.

He was so tired that he flopped down upon the nice soft sand on the floor of the rabbit-hole and shut his eyes. His mother was busy cooking; she wondered what he had done with his clothes. It was the second little jacket and pair of shoes that Peter had lost in a fortnight!

I am sorry to say that Peter was not very well during the evening.

His mother put him to bed, and made some camomile tea; and she gave a dose of it to Peter!

"One table-spoonful to be taken at bed-time."

But Flopsy, Mopsy, and Cotton-tail had bread and milk and black-berries for supper.

THE END

The Tale of Benjamin Bunny

1904

About This Book

The real-life Benjamin Bunny was a tame rabbit of Beatrix Potter's, whom she sketched constantly, and whose exploits continually amused her. "He is an abject coward, but believes in bluster, could stare our old dog out of countenance, chase a cat that has turned tail." Although Benjamin had died by 1904, when this story was published, Beatrix may well have been thinking of him when she created Peter Rabbit's cousin, Benjamin. Little Benjamin is a very self-possessed animal, who makes himself quite at home in Mr. McGregor's garden.

Beatrix sketched background scenes for the tale while on holiday in Fawe Park, a house with a beautiful garden in the Lake District. The book is dedicated to "the children of Sawrey from Old Mr. Bunny." Beatrix was later to settle in the Lake District village of Sawrey, buying a small farm there in 1905.

ONE morning a little rabbit sat on a bank. He pricked his ears and listened to the trit-trot, trit-trot of a pony.

A gig was coming along the road; it was driven by Mr. McGregor, and beside him sat Mrs. McGregor in her best bonnet.

As soon as they had passed, little Benjamin Bunny slid down into the road, and set off—with a hop, skip and a jump—to call upon his relations, who lived in the wood at the back of Mr. McGregor's garden.

That wood was full of rabbit holes; and in the neatest sandiest hole of all, lived Benjamin's aunt and his cousins—Flopsy, Mopsy, Cotton-tail and Peter.

Old Mrs. Rabbit was a widow; she earned her living by knitting rabbit-wool mittens and muffetees (I once bought a pair at a bazaar). She also sold herbs, and rosemary tea, and rabbit-tobacco (which is what *we* call lavender).

Little Benjamin did not very much want to see his Aunt.

He came round the back of the fir-tree, and nearly tumbled upon the top of his Cousin Peter.

Peter was sitting by himself. He looked poorly, and was dressed in a red cotton pocket-handkerchief.

"Peter,"—said little Benjamin, in a whisper—"who has got your clothes?"

Peter replied—"The scarecrow in Mr. McGregor's garden," and described how he had been chased about the garden, and had dropped his shoes and coat.

Little Benjamin sat down beside his cousin, and assured him that Mr. McGregor had gone out in a gig, and Mrs. McGregor also; and certainly for the day, because she was wearing her best bonnet.

Peter said he hoped that it would rain.

At this point, old Mrs. Rabbit's voice was heard inside the rabbit hole, calling—"Cotton-tail! Cotton-tail! Fetch some more camomile!"

Peter said he thought he might feel better if he went for a walk.

They went away hand in hand, and got upon the flat top of the wall at the bottom of the wood. From here they looked down into Mr. McGregor's garden. Peter's coat and shoes were plainly to be seen upon the scare-crow, topped with an old tam-o-shanter of Mr. McGregor's.

Little Benjamin said, "It spoils people's clothes to squeeze under a gate; the proper way to get in, is to climb down a pear tree."

Peter fell down head first; but it was of no consequence, as the bed below was newly raked and quite soft.

It had been sown with lettuces.

They left a great many odd little foot-marks all over the bed, especially little Benjamin, who was wearing clogs.

Little Benjamin said that the first thing to be done was to get back Peter's clothes, in order that they might be able to use the pocket-handkerchief.

They took them off the scarecrow. There had been rain during the night; there was water in the shoes, and the coat was somewhat shrunk.

Benjamin tried on the tam-o-shanter, but it was too big for him.

Then he suggested that they should fill the pocket-handkerchief with onions, as a little present for his Aunt.

Peter did not seem to be enjoying himself; he kept hearing noises.

Benjamin, on the contrary, was perfectly at home, and ate a lettuce leaf. He said that he was in the habit of coming to the garden with his father to get lettuces for their Sunday dinner.

(The name of little Benjamin's papa was old Mr. Benjamin Bunny.)

The lettuces certainly were very fine.

Peter did not eat anything; he said he should like to go home. Presently he dropped half the onions.

Little Benjamin said that it was not possible to get back up the pear-tree, with a load of vegetables. He led the way boldly towards the other end of the garden. They went along a little walk on planks, under a sunny red-brick wall.

The mice sat on their door-steps cracking cherry-stones, they winked at Peter Rabbit and little Benjamin Bunny.

Presently Peter let the pocket-handkerchief go again.

They got amongst flowerpots, and frames and tubs; Peter heard noises worse than ever, his eyes were as big as lolly-pops!

He was a step or two in front of his cousin, when he suddenly stopped.

This is what those little rabbits saw round that corner!

Little Benjamin took one look, and then, in half a minute less than no time, he hid himself and Peter and the onions underneath a large basket . . .

The cat got up and stretched herself, and came and sniffed at the basket.

Perhaps she liked the smell of onions!

Anyway, she sat down upon the top of the basket.

She sat there for *five hours*.

*   *   *

I cannot draw you a picture of Peter and Benjamin underneath the basket, because it was quite dark, and because the smell of onions was fearful; it made Peter Rabbit and little Benjamin cry.

The sun got round behind the wood, and it was quite late in the afternoon; but still the cat sat upon the basket.

At length there was a pitter-patter, pitter-patter, and some bits of mortar fell from the wall above.

The cat looked up and saw old Mr. Benjamin Bunny prancing along the top of the wall of the upper terrace.

He was smoking a pipe of rabbit-tobacco, and had a little switch in his hand.

He was looking for his son.

Old Mr. Bunny had no opinion whatever of cats.

He took a tremendous jump off the top of the wall on to the top of the cat, and cuffed it off the basket, and kicked it into the green-house, scratching off a handful of fur.

The cat was too much surprised to scratch back.

When old Mr. Bunny had driven the cat into the green-house, he locked the door.

Then he came back to the basket and took out his son Benjamin by the ears, and whipped him with the little switch.

Then he took out his nephew Peter.

Then he took out the handkerchief of onions, and marched out of the garden.

When Mr. McGregor returned about half an hour later, he observed several things which perplexed him.

It looked as though some person had been walking all over the garden in a pair of clogs—only the foot-marks were too ridiculously little!

Also he could not understand how the cat could have managed to shut herself up *inside* the green-house, locking the door upon the *outside*.

When Peter got home, his mother forgave him, because she was so glad to see that he had found his shoes and coat. Cotton-tail and Peter folded up the pocket-handkerchief, and old Mrs. Rabbit strung up the onions and hung them from the kitchen ceiling, with the bunches of herbs and the rabbit-tobacco.

THE END

The Tale of The Flopsy Bunnies

1909

About This Book

The Tale of The Flopsy Bunnies pays another visit to the world of Peter Rabbit and Benjamin Bunny. Both rabbits have now grown up, Benjamin has married Peter's sister Flopsy and although still "improvident and cheerful", has a large family to care for. Beatrix Potter was well aware that her earlier books had created a huge demand for rabbit stories, and dedicated this one, "For all little friends of Mr. McGregor and Peter and Benjamin." Besides, she enjoyed painting rabbits, and gardens too. When preparing the book in 1909 she was staying with her uncle Fred and aunt Harriet Burton at Gwaynynog, their large house in Wales, and made many studies of the garden there. She described it on an earlier visit as "the prettiest kind of garden, where bright old-fashioned flowers grow amongst the currant bushes." It is beautifully depicted in her lovely illustrations.

IT is said that the effect of eating too much lettuce is "soporific".

I have never felt sleepy after eating lettuces; but then *I* am not a rabbit.

They certainly had a very soporific effect upon the Flopsy Bunnies!

When Benjamin Bunny grew up, he married his Cousin Flopsy. They had a large family, and they were very improvident and cheerful.

I do not remember the separate names of their children; they were generally called the "Flopsy Bunnies".

As there was not always quite enough to eat—Benjamin used to borrow cabbages from Flopsy's brother, Peter Rabbit, who kept a nursery garden.

Sometimes Peter Rabbit had no cabbages to spare.

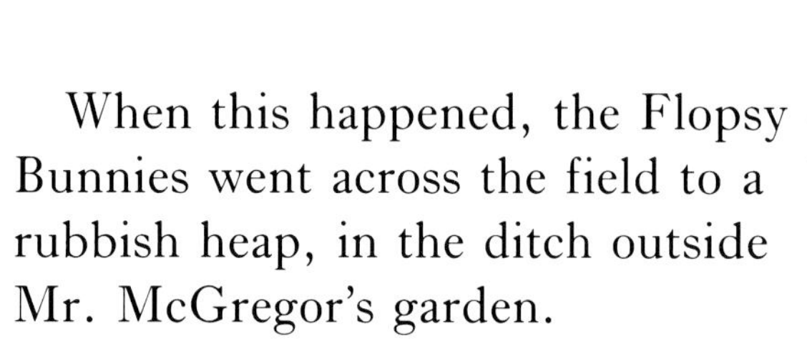

When this happened, the Flopsy Bunnies went across the field to a rubbish heap, in the ditch outside Mr. McGregor's garden.

Mr. McGregor's rubbish heap was a mixture. There were jam pots and paper bags, and mountains of chopped grass from the mowing machine (which always tasted oily), and some rotten vegetable marrows and an old boot or two. One day—oh joy!—there were a quantity of overgrown lettuces, which had "shot" into flower.

The Flopsy Bunnies simply stuffed lettuces. By degrees, one after another, they were overcome with slumber, and lay down in the mown grass.

Benjamin was not so much overcome as his children. Before going to sleep he was sufficiently wide awake to put a paper bag over his head to keep off the flies.

The little Flopsy Bunnies slept delightfully in the warm sun. From the lawn beyond the garden came the distant clacketty sound of the mowing machine. The blue-bottles buzzed about the wall, and a little old mouse picked over the rubbish among the jam pots.

(I can tell you her name, she was called Thomasina Tittlemouse, a woodmouse with a long tail.)

She rustled across the paper bag, and awakened Benjamin Bunny.

The mouse apologized profusely, and said that she knew Peter Rabbit.

While she and Benjamin were talking, close under the wall, they heard a heavy tread above their heads; and suddenly Mr. McGregor emptied out a sackful of lawn mowings right upon the top of the sleeping Flopsy Bunnies! Benjamin shrank down under his paper bag. The mouse hid in a jam pot.

The little rabbits smiled sweetly in their sleep under the shower of grass; they did not awake because the lettuces had been so soporific.

They dreamt that their mother Flopsy was tucking them up in a hay bed.

Mr. McGregor looked down after emptying his sack. He saw some funny little brown tips of ears sticking up through the lawn mowings. He stared at them for some time.

Presently a fly settled on one of them and it moved.

Mr. McGregor climbed down on to the rubbish heap—

"One, two, three, four! five! six leetle rabbits!" said he as he dropped them into his sack.

The Flopsy Bunnies dreamt that their mother was turning them over in bed. They stirred a little in their sleep, but still they did not wake up.

Mr. McGregor tied up the sack and left it on the wall.

He went to put away the mowing machine.

While he was gone, Mrs. Flopsy Bunny (who had remained at home) came across the field.

She looked suspiciously at the sack and wondered where everybody was?

Then the mouse came out of her jam pot, and Benjamin took the paper bag off his head, and they told the doleful tale.

Benjamin and Flopsy were in despair, they could not undo the string.

But Mrs. Tittlemouse was a resourceful person. She nibbled a hole in the bottom corner of the sack.

The little rabbits were pulled out and pinched to wake them.

Their parents stuffed the empty sack with three rotten vegetable marrows, an old blacking-brush and two decayed turnips.

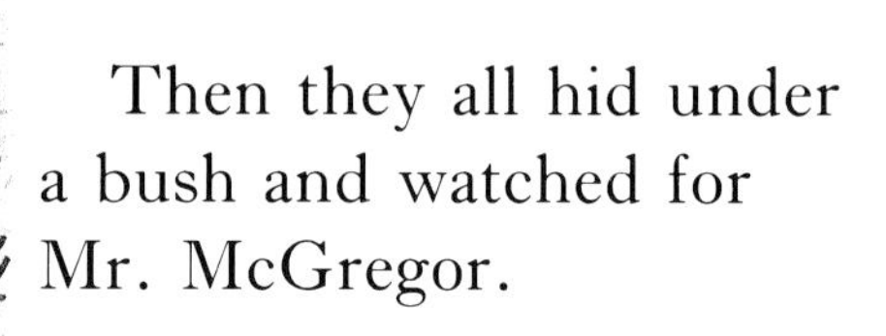

Then they all hid under a bush and watched for Mr. McGregor.

Mr. McGregor came back and picked up the sack, and carried it off.

He carried it hanging down, as if it were rather heavy.

The Flopsy Bunnies followed at a safe distance.

They watched him go into his house.

And then they crept up to the window to listen.

Mr. McGregor threw down the sack on the stone floor in a way that would have been extremely painful to the Flopsy Bunnies, if they had happened to have been inside it.

They could hear him drag his chair on the flags, and chuckle—

"One, two, three, four, five, six leetle rabbits!" said Mr. McGregor.

"Eh? What's that? What have they been spoiling now?" inquired Mrs. McGregor.

"One, two, three, four, five, six leetle fat rabbits!" repeated Mr. McGregor, counting on his fingers—"one, two, three—"

"Don't you be silly; what do you mean, you silly old man?"

"In the sack! One, two, three, four, five, six!" replied Mr. McGregor.

(The youngest Flopsy Bunny got upon the window-sill.)

Mrs. McGregor took hold of the sack and felt it. She said she could feel six, but they must be *old* rabbits, because they were so hard and all different shapes.

"Not fit to eat; but the skins will do fine to line my old cloak."

"Line your old cloak?" shouted Mr. McGregor—"I shall sell them and buy myself baccy!"

"Rabbit tobacco! I shall skin them and cut off their heads."

Mrs. McGregor untied the sack and put her hand inside.

When she felt the vegetables she became very very angry. She said that Mr. McGregor had "done it a purpose".

And Mr. McGregor was very angry too. One of the rotten marrows came flying through the kitchen window, and hit the youngest Flopsy Bunny.

It was rather hurt.

Then Benjamin and Flopsy thought that it was time to go home.

So Mr. McGregor did not get his tobacco, and Mrs. McGregor did not get her rabbit skins.

But next Christmas Thomasina Tittlemouse got a present of enough rabbit-wool to make herself a cloak and a hood, and a handsome muff and a pair of warm mittens.

THE END

THE TALE OF MRS. TITTLEMOUSE

1910

About This Book

Beatrix Potter's interest in all kinds of creatures, from spiders to bees, is clearly evident in *The Tale of Mrs. Tittlemouse*. There are no people in the story, but all sorts of creepy-crawly characters invade Mrs. Tittlemouse's tidy home. Originally, Beatrix had woodlice, an earwig and a centipede among the uninvited guests, but her publishers felt the first two insects were unsuitable for a children's book! Beatrix herself decided against the centipede, replacing it with a most beautiful picture of Miss Butterfly tasting the sugar. She evidently bore no grudge against her editor for the alterations he requested, for the book is dedicated to Harold Warne's daughter Nellie, who also received the manuscript as a New Year's present.

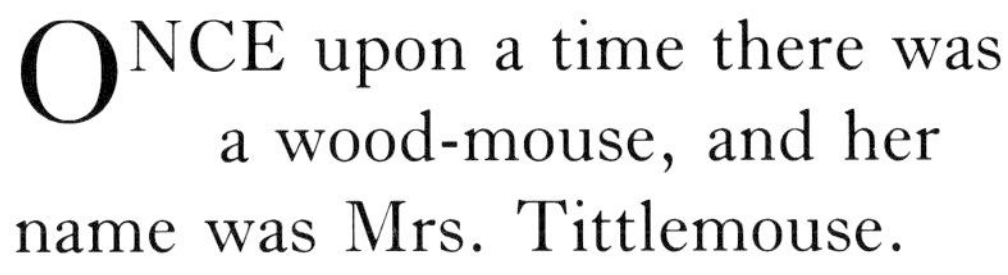

ONCE upon a time there was a wood-mouse, and her name was Mrs. Tittlemouse.

She lived in a bank under a hedge.

Such a funny house!

There were yards and yards of sandy passages, leading to storerooms and nut-cellars and seed-cellars, all amongst the roots of the hedge.

There was a kitchen, a parlour, a pantry, and a larder.

Also, there was Mrs. Tittlemouse's bedroom, where she slept in a little box bed!

Mrs. Tittlemouse was a most terribly tidy particular little mouse, always sweeping and dusting the soft sandy floors.

Sometimes a beetle lost its way in the passages.

"Shuh! shuh! little dirty feet!" said Mrs. Tittlemouse, clattering her dust-pan.

And one day a little old woman ran up and down in a red spotty cloak.

"Your house is on fire, Mother Ladybird! Fly away home to your children!"

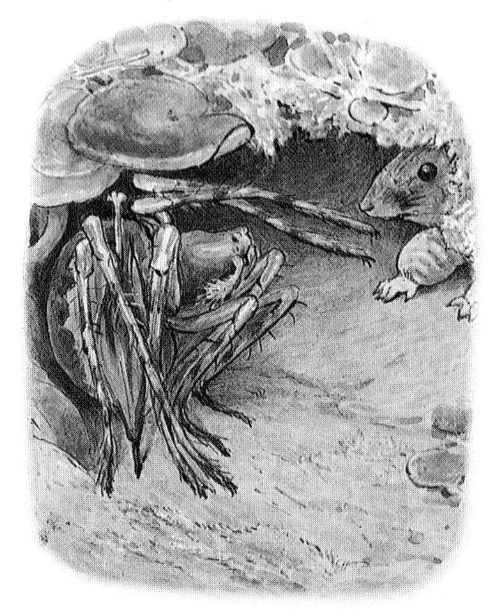

Another day, a big fat spider came in to shelter from the rain.

"Beg pardon, is this not Miss Muffet's?"

"Go away, you bold bad spider! Leaving ends of cobweb all over my nice clean house!"

She bundled the spider out at a window.

He let himself down the hedge with a long thin bit of string.

Mrs. Tittlemouse went on her way to a distant storeroom, to fetch cherry-stones and thistle-down seed for dinner.

All along the passage she sniffed, and looked at the floor.

"I smell a smell of honey; is it the cowslips outside, in the hedge?

I am sure I can see the marks of little dirty feet."

Suddenly round a corner, she met Babbitty Bumble—"Zizz, Bizz, Bizzz!" said the bumble bee.

Mrs. Tittlemouse looked at her severely. She wished that she had a broom.

"Good-day, Babbitty Bumble; I should be glad to buy some beeswax. But what are you doing down here?

Why do you always come in at a window, and say 'Zizz, Bizz, Bizzz'?" Mrs. Tittlemouse began to get cross.

"Zizz, Wizz, Wizzz!" replied Babbitty Bumble in a peevish squeak. She sidled down a passage, and disappeared into a storeroom which had been used for acorns.

Mrs. Tittlemouse had eaten the acorns before Christmas; the storeroom ought to have been empty.

But it was full of untidy dry moss.

Mrs. Tittlemouse began to pull out the moss. Three or four other bees put their heads out, and buzzed fiercely.

"I am not in the habit of letting lodgings; this is an intrusion!" said Mrs. Tittlemouse. "I will have them turned out—"

"Buzz! Buzz! Buzzz!"

—"I wonder who would help me?"

"Bizz, Wizz, Wizzz!"

—"I will not have Mr. Jackson; he never wipes his feet."

Mrs. Tittlemouse decided to leave the bees till after dinner.

When she got back to the parlour, she heard someone coughing in a fat voice; and there sat Mr. Jackson himself!

He was sitting all over a small rocking-chair, twiddling his thumbs and smiling, with his feet on the fender.

He lived in a drain below the hedge, in a very dirty wet ditch.

"How do you do, Mr. Jackson? Deary me, you have got very wet!"

"Thank you, thank you, thank you, Mrs. Tittlemouse! I'll sit awhile and dry myself," said Mr. Jackson.

He sat and smiled, and the water dripped off his coat tails. Mrs. Tittlemouse went round with a mop.

He sat such a while that he had to be asked if he would take some dinner?

First she offered him cherry-stones. "Thank you, thank you, Mrs. Tittlemouse! No teeth, no teeth, no teeth!" said Mr. Jackson.

He opened his mouth most unnecessarily wide; he certainly had not a tooth in his head.

Then she offered him thistle-down seed—"Tiddly, widdly, widdly! Pouff, pouff, puff!" said Mr. Jackson. He blew the thistle-down all over the room.

"Thank you, thank you, thank you, Mrs. Tittlemouse! Now what I really—*really* should like—would be a little dish of honey!"

"I am afraid I have not got any, Mr. Jackson," said Mrs. Tittlemouse.

"Tiddly, widdly, widdly, Mrs. Tittlemouse!" said the smiling Mr. Jackson, "I can *smell* it; that is why I came to call."

Mr. Jackson rose ponderously from the table, and began to look into the cupboards.

Mrs. Tittlemouse followed him with a dish-cloth, to wipe his large wet footmarks off the parlour floor.

When he had convinced himself that there was no honey in the cupboards, he began to walk down the passage.

"Indeed, indeed, you will stick fast, Mr. Jackson!"

"Tiddly, widdly, widdly, Mrs. Tittlemouse!"

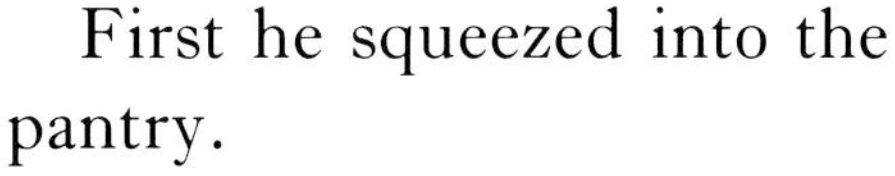

First he squeezed into the pantry.

"Tiddly, widdly, widdly? No honey? No honey, Mrs. Tittlemouse?"

There were three creepy-crawly people hiding in the plate-rack. Two of them got away; but the littlest one he caught.

Then he squeezed into the larder. Miss Butterfly was tasting the sugar; but she flew away out of the window.

"Tiddly, widdly, widdly, Mrs. Tittlemouse; you seem to have plenty of visitors!"

"And without any invitation!" said Mrs. Thomasina Tittlemouse.

They went along the sandy passage—"Tiddly widdly—" "Buzz! Wizz! Wizz!"

He met Babbitty round a corner, and snapped her up, and put her down again.

"I do not like bumble bees. They are all over bristles," said Mr. Jackson, wiping his mouth with his coat-sleeve.

"Get out, you nasty old toad!" shrieked Babbitty Bumble.

"I shall go distracted!" scolded Mrs. Tittlemouse.

She shut herself up in the nut-cellar while Mr. Jackson pulled out the bees-nest. He seemed to have no objection to stings.

When Mrs. Tittlemouse ventured to come out—everybody had gone away.

But the untidiness was something dreadful—"Never did I see such a mess—smears of honey; and moss, and thistle-down—and marks of big and little dirty feet—all over my nice clean house!"

She gathered up the moss and the remains of the beeswax.

Then she went out and fetched some twigs, to partly close up the front door.

"I will make it too small for Mr. Jackson!"

She fetched soft soap, and flannel, and a new scrubbing brush from the storeroom. But she was too tired to do any more.

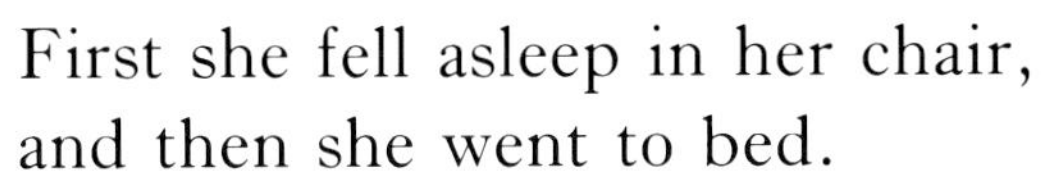

First she fell asleep in her chair, and then she went to bed.

"Will it ever be tidy again?" said poor Mrs. Tittlemouse.

Next morning she got up very early and began a spring cleaning which lasted a fortnight.

She swept, and scrubbed, and dusted; and she rubbed up the furniture with beeswax, and polished her little tin spoons.

When it was all beautifully neat and clean, she gave a party to five other little mice, without Mr. Jackson.

He smelt the party and came up the bank, but he could not squeeze in at the door.

So they handed him out acorn-cupfuls of honey-dew through the window, and he was not at all offended.

He sat outside in the sun, and said—"Tiddly, widdly, widdly! Your very good health, Mrs. Tittlemouse!"

THE END

THE TAILOR OF GLOUCESTER

1903

"I'LL BE AT CHARGES FOR A LOOKING-GLASS;
AND ENTERTAIN A SCORE OR TWO OF TAILORS."
Richard III

About This Book

The Tailor of Gloucester was Beatrix Potter's own favourite among all her books. She first heard the true story on which it is based when visiting her cousin, Caroline Hutton, who lived near Gloucester. Leaving an unfinished waistcoat for the Mayor of Gloucester in his shop one Saturday morning, a tailor was amazed to find it ready on the Monday, except for one buttonhole, for which there was "no more twist". In reality, his two assistants had secretly completed the job, but Beatrix Potter has the work finished by little brown mice. She adds an extra note of enchantment by setting the story on Christmas Eve, when animals can talk, and weaving in many of her favourite traditional rhymes. The book was dedicated to another of the Moore children, this time to Freda, "because you are fond of fairy-tales, and have been ill."

IN the time of swords and periwigs and full-skirted coats with flowered lappets—when gentlemen wore ruffles, and gold-laced waist-coats of paduasoy and taffeta—there lived a tailor in Gloucester.

He sat in the window of a little shop in Westgate Street, cross-legged on a table, from morning till dark.

All day long while the light lasted he sewed and snippeted, piecing out his satin and pompadour, and lute-string; stuffs had strange names, and were very expensive in the days of the Tailor of Gloucester.

But although he sewed fine silk for his neighbours, he himself was very, very poor—a little old man in spectacles, with a pinched face, old crooked fingers, and a suit of thread-bare clothes.

He cut his coats without waste, according to his embroidered cloth; they were very small ends and snippets that lay about upon the table—"Too narrow breadths for nought—except waistcoats for mice," said the tailor.

One bitter cold day near Christmas-time the tailor began to make a coat—a coat of cherry-coloured corded silk embroidered with pansies and roses, and a cream-coloured satin waistcoat—trimmed with gauze and green worsted chenille—for the Mayor of Gloucester.

The tailor worked and worked, and he talked to himself. He measured the silk, and turned it round and round, and trimmed it into shape with his shears; the table was all littered with cherry-coloured snippets.

"No breadth at all, and cut on the cross; it is no breadth at all; tippets for mice and ribbons for mobs! for mice!" said the Tailor of Gloucester.

When the snow-flakes came down against the small leaded window-panes and shut out the light, the tailor had done his day's work; all the silk and satin lay cut out upon the table.

There were twelve pieces for the coat and four pieces for the waistcoat; and there were pocket flaps and cuffs, and buttons all in order. For the lining of the coat there was fine yellow taffeta; and for the button-holes of the waist-coat, there was cherry-coloured twist. And everything was ready to sew together in the morning, all measured and sufficient—except that there was wanting just one single skein of cherry-coloured twisted silk.

The tailor came out of his shop at dark, for he did not sleep there at nights; he fastened the window

and locked the door, and took away the key. No one lived there at night but little brown mice, and they run in and out without any keys!

For behind the wooden wainscots of all the old houses in Gloucester, there are little mouse staircases and secret trap-doors; and the mice run from house to house through those long narrow passages; they can run all over the town without going into the streets.

But the tailor came out of his shop, and shuffled home through the snow. He lived quite near by in College Court, next the doorway to College Green; and although it was not a big house, the tailor was so poor he only rented the kitchen.

He lived alone with his cat; it was called Simpkin.

Now all day long while the tailor was out at work, Simpkin kept house by himself; and he also was fond of the mice, though he gave them no satin for coats!

"Miaw?" said the cat when the tailor opened the door. "Miaw?"

The tailor replied—"Simpkin, we shall make our fortune, but I am worn to a ravelling. Take this groat (which is our last fourpence) and Simpkin, take a china pipkin; buy a penn'orth of bread, a penn'orth of milk and a penn'orth of sausages. And oh, Simpkin, with the last penny of our fourpence buy me one penn'orth of cherry-coloured silk. But do not lose the last penny of the fourpence, Simpkin, or I am undone and worn to a thread-paper, for I have NO MORE TWIST."

Then Simpkin again said, "Miaw?" and took the groat and the pipkin, and went out into the dark.

The tailor was very tired and beginning to be ill. He sat down by the hearth and talked to himself about that wonderful coat.

"I shall make my fortune—to be cut bias—the Mayor of Gloucester is to be married on Christmas Day in the morning, and he hath ordered a coat and an embroidered waistcoat—to be lined with yellow taffeta—and the taffeta sufficeth; there is no more left over in snippets than will serve to make tippets for mice—"

Then the tailor started; for suddenly, interrupting him, from the dresser at the other side of the kitchen came a number of little noises—

Tip tap, tip tap, tip tap tip!

"Now what can that be?" said the Tailor of Gloucester, jumping up from his chair. The dresser was covered with crockery and pipkins,

willow pattern plates, and tea-cups and mugs.

The tailor crossed the kitchen, and stood quite still beside the dresser, listening, and peering through his spectacles. Again from under a tea-cup, came those funny little noises—

Tip tap, tip tap, tip tap tip!

"This is very peculiar," said the Tailor of Gloucester; and he lifted up the tea-cup which was upside down. Out stepped a little live lady mouse, and made a curtsey to the tailor! Then she hopped away down off the dresser, and under the wainscot.

The tailor sat down again by the fire, warming his poor cold hands, and mumbling to himself—

"The waistcoat is cut out from peach-coloured satin—tambour stitch and rose-buds in beautiful floss silk. Was I wise to entrust my last fourpence to Simpkin? One-and-twenty button-holes of cherry-coloured twist!"

But all at once, from the dresser, there came other little noises:

Tip tap, tip tap, tip tap tip!

"This is passing extraordinary!" said the Tailor of Gloucester, and turned over another tea-cup, which was upside down. Out stepped a little gentleman mouse, and made a bow to the tailor!

And then from all over the dresser came a chorus of little tappings, all sounding together, and answering one another, like watch-beetles in an old worm-eaten window-shutter—

Tip tap, tip tap, tip tap tip!

And out from under tea-cups and from under bowls and basins, stepped other and more little mice who hopped away down off the dresser and under the wainscot.

The tailor sat down, close over the fire, lamenting—"One-and-twenty button-holes of cherry-coloured silk! To be finished by noon of Saturday: and this is Tuesday evening. Was it right to let loose those mice, undoubtedly the property of Simpkin? Alack, I am undone, for I have no more twist!"

The little mice came out again, and listened to the tailor; they took notice of the pattern of that wonderful coat. They whispered to one another about the taffeta lining, and about little mouse tippets.

And then all at once they all ran away together down the passage behind the wainscot, squeaking and calling to one another, as they ran from house to house; and not one mouse was left in the tailor's kitchen when Simpkin came back with the pipkin of milk!

Simpkin opened the door and bounced in, with an angry "G-r-r-miaw!" like a cat that is vexed: for he hated the snow, and there was snow in his ears, and snow in his collar at the back of his neck. He put down the loaf and the sausages upon the dresser, and sniffed.

"Simpkin," said the tailor, "where is my twist?"

But Simpkin set down the pipkin of milk upon the dresser, and looked suspiciously at the tea-cups. He wanted his supper of little fat mouse!

"Simpkin," said the tailor, "where is my TWIST?"

But Simpkin hid a little parcel privately in the tea-pot, and spit and growled at the tailor; and if Simpkin had been able to talk, he would have asked: "Where is my MOUSE?"

"Alack, I am undone!" said the Tailor of Gloucester, and went sadly to bed.

All that night long Simpkin hunted and searched through the kitchen, peeping into cupboards and under the wainscot, and into the tea-pot where he had hidden that twist; but still he found never a mouse!

Whenever the tailor muttered and talked in his sleep, Simpkin said "Miaw-ger-r-w-s-s-ch!" and made strange horrid noises, as cats do at night.

For the poor old tailor was very ill with a fever, tossing and turning in his four-post bed; and still in his dreams he mumbled—"No more twist! No more twist!"

All that day he was ill, and the next day, and the next; and what should become of the cherry-coloured coat? In the tailor's shop in Westgate Street the embroidered silk and satin lay cut out upon the table—one-and-twenty button-holes—and who should come to sew them, when the window was barred, and the door was fast locked?

But that does not hinder the little brown mice; they run in and out without any keys through all the old houses in Gloucester!

Out of doors the market folks went trudging through the snow to buy their geese and turkeys, and to bake their Christmas pies; but there would be no Christmas dinner for Simpkin and the poor old Tailor of Gloucester.

The tailor lay ill for three days and nights; and then it was Christmas Eve, and very late at night. The moon climbed up over the roofs and chimneys, and looked down over the gateway into College Court. There were no lights in the windows, nor any sound in the houses; all the city of Gloucester was fast asleep under the snow.

And still Simpkin wanted his mice, and he mewed as he stood beside the four-post bed.

But it is in the old story that all the beasts can talk, in the night between Christmas Eve and Christmas Day in the morning (though there are very few folk that can hear them, or know what it is that they say).

When the Cathedral clock struck twelve there was an answer—like an echo of the chimes—and Simpkin heard it, and came out of the tailor's door, and wandered about in the snow.

From all the roofs and gables and old wooden houses in Gloucester came a thousand merry voices singing the old Christmas rhymes—all the old songs that ever I heard of, and some that I don't know, like Whittington's bells.

First and loudest the cocks cried out: "Dame, get up, and bake your pies!"

"Oh, dilly, dilly, dilly!" sighed Simpkin.

And now in a garret there were lights and sounds of dancing, and cats came from over the way.

"Hey, diddle, diddle, the cat and the fiddle! All the cats in Gloucester—except me," said Simpkin.

Under the wooden eaves the starlings and sparrows sang of Christmas pies; the jack-daws woke up in the Cathedral tower; and although it was the middle of the night the throstles and robins sang; the air was quite full of little twittering tunes.

But it was all rather provoking to poor hungry Simpkin!

Particularly he was vexed with some little shrill voices from behind a wooden lattice. I think that they

were bats, because they always have very small voices—especially in a black frost, when they talk in their sleep, like the Tailor of Gloucester.

They said something mysterious that sounded like—

"Buz, quoth the blue fly; hum, quoth the bee;
Buz and hum they cry, and so do we!"

and Simpkin went away shaking his ears as if he had a bee in his bonnet.

From the tailor's shop in Westgate came a glow of light; and when Simpkin crept up to peep in at the window it was full of candles. There was a snippeting of scissors, and snappeting of thread; and little mouse voices sang loudly and gaily—

"Four-and-twenty tailors
Went to catch a snail,
The best man amongst them
Durst not touch her tail;
She put out her horns
Like a little kyloe cow,
Run, tailors, run! or she'll have you all e'en now!"

Then without a pause the little mouse voices went on again—

"Sieve my lady's oatmeal,
Grind my lady's flour,
Put it in a chestnut,
Let it stand an hour—"

"Mew! Mew!" interrupted Simpkin, and he scratched at the door.

But the key was under the tailor's pillow, he could not get in.

The little mice only laughed, and tried another tune—

"Three little mice sat down to spin,
Pussy passed by and she peeped in.
What are you at, my fine little men?
Making coats for gentlemen.
Shall I come in and cut off your threads?
Oh, no, Miss Pussy, you'd bite off
our heads!"

"Mew! Mew!" cried Simpkin.

"Hey diddle dinketty?" answered the little mice—

"Hey diddle dinketty, poppetty pet!
The merchants of London they wear
scarlet;
Silk in the collar, and gold in the hem,
So merrily march the merchantmen!"

They clicked their thimbles to mark the time, but none of the songs pleased Simpkin; he sniffed and mewed at the door of the shop.

"And then I bought
A pipkin and a popkin,
A slipkin and a slopkin,
All for one farthing—

—and upon the kitchen dresser!" added the rude little mice.

"Mew! scratch! scratch!" scuffled Simpkin on the window-sill; while the little mice inside sprang to their feet, and all began to shout at once in little twittering voices: "No more twist! No more twist!" And they barred up the window shutters and shut out Simpkin.

But still through the nicks in the shutters he could hear the click of thimbles, and little mouse voices singing—

"No more twist! No more twist!"

Simpkin came away from his shop and went home, considering in his mind. He found the poor old tailor without fever, sleeping peacefully.

Then Simpkin went on tip-toe and took a little parcel of silk out of the tea-pot, and looked at it in the moonlight; and he felt quite ashamed of his badness compared with those good little mice!

When the tailor awoke in the morning, the first thing which he saw upon the patchwork quilt, was a skein of cherry-coloured twisted silk, and beside his bed stood the repentant Simpkin!

"Alack, I am worn to a ravelling," said the Tailor of Gloucester, "but I have my twist!"

The sun was shining on the snow when the tailor got up and dressed, and came out into the street with Simpkin running before him.

The starlings whistled on the chimney stacks, and the throstles and robins sang—but they sang their own little noises, not the words they had sung in the night.

"Alack," said the tailor, "I have

my twist; but no more strength—nor time—than will serve to make me one single button-hole; for this is Christmas Day in the Morning! The Mayor of Gloucester shall be married by noon—and where is his cherry-coloured coat?"

He unlocked the door of the little shop in Westgate Street, and Simpkin ran in, like a cat that expects something.

But there was no one there! Not even one little brown mouse!

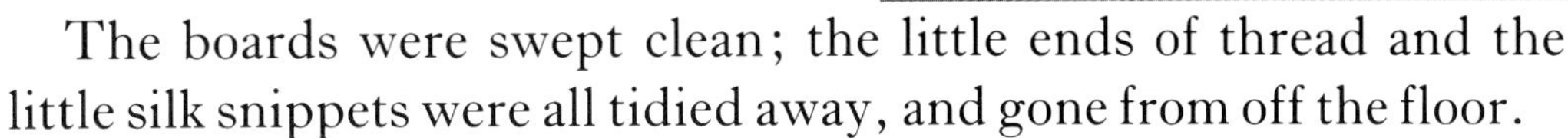

The boards were swept clean; the little ends of thread and the little silk snippets were all tidied away, and gone from off the floor.

But upon the table—oh joy! the tailor gave a shout—there, where he had left plain cuttings of silk—there lay the most beautifullest coat and embroidered satin waistcoat that ever were worn by a Mayor of Gloucester.

There were roses and pansies upon the facings of the coat; and the waistcoat was worked with poppies and corn-flowers.

Everything was finished except just one single cherry-coloured button-hole, and where that button-hole was wanting there was pinned a scrap of paper with these words—in little teeny weeny writing—

NO MORE TWIST

And from then began the luck of the Tailor of Gloucester; he grew quite stout, and he grew quite rich.

He made the most wonderful waistcoats for all the rich merchants of Gloucester, and for all the fine gentlemen of the country round.

Never were seen such ruffles, or such embroidered cuffs and lappets! But his button-holes were the greatest triumph of it all.

The stitches of those button-holes were so neat—*so* neat—I wonder how they could be stitched by an old man in spectacles, with crooked old fingers, and a tailor's thimble.

The stitches of those button-holes were so small—*so* small—they looked as if they had been made by little mice!

THE END